The Last Chance Dance and Other Adventures

Candace McNaughton-Stuart

Mosaic Press
Oakville, ON. - Buffalo, N.Y.

Canadian Cataloguing in Publication Data

McNaughton-Stuart, Candace, 1951-
    The last chance dance and other adventures

Poems.
ISBN 0-88962-594-8

1. Children's poetry, Canadian (English).*
I. Title.

PS8575.N39L3 1995   jC811'.54   C95-932936-6
PZ8.3.M35La 1995

No part of this book may be reproduced or transmitted in any form, by any means, electronic or mechanical, including photocopying and recording information storage and retrieval systems, without permission in writing from the publisher, except by a reviewer who may quote brief passages in a review.

Published by MOSAIC PRESS, P.O. Box 1032, Oakville, Ontario, L6J 5E9, Canada. Offices and warehouse at 1252 Speers Road, Units #1&2, Oakville, Ontario, L6L 5N9, Canada and Mosaic Press, 85 River Rock Drive, Suite 202, Buffalo, N.Y., 14207, USA.

Mosaic Press acknowledges the assistance of the Canada Council, the Ontario Arts Council, the Ontario Ministry of Culture, Tourism and Recreation and the Dept. of Canadian Heritage, Government of Canada, for their support of our publishing programme.

Copyright © Candace McNaughton-Stuart, 1996

Cover and book design by Susan Parker
Printed and bound in Canada
ISBN 0-88962-594-8

In Canada:
MOSAIC PRESS, 1252 Speers Road, Units #1&2, Oakville, Ontario, L6L 5N9, Canada. P.O. Box 1032, Oakville, Ontario, L6J 5E9
In the United States:
MOSAIC PRESS, 85 River Rock Drive, Suite 202, Buffalo, N.Y., 14207
In the UK and Western Europe:
DRAKE INTERNATIONAL SERVICES, Market House, Market Place, Deddington, Oxford. OX15 OSF

The Author

Candace McNaughton-Stuart presents *The Last Chance Dance and Other Adventures* her second collection of poems to appeal to children aged four to eight. Her poems are completely fresh and delightful creating convincing poetic representations of the world of childhood. Her first book *The Chicken Tree & Other Fevers* also celebrates her talent.

The Illustrators

Michael Bernhardt, Ryan Stuart, Nikki Little, Chris Travaglini, Michael Little, Melisa Celebi, Serena Smith, Harun Celebi and Harold Warburton

* the two small pen & ink Landscapes are approximately 75 years old: by Harold 'Perks' Warburton. He was the father of Teady & Perks

Table of Contents

Jehosaphat 1
The Last Chance Dance 5
My Best Castle 9
Static Cling 12
Teddy and Perks 15
Gizzard Skinning Time 18
Our Tea Party 22
When Ooffie Met Lion 25
Stitches 31
The Contest 35
Carolyn's Scary Story 38
The Catch 42
When Gordie Went to Sea 45
Down Yi 50
One More Time 54
Pogo 55
The Mission 60

Jehosaphat

Jehosaphat was a turkey
and we fed him grits and corn.
We thought we'd plump him up
quite large
and serve him on a leafy barge
with sweet potatoes warm.
And we liked to visit often
as he poked and pecked around.
We'd toss him hands of seeds and nuts
and watch him gobble and gobble
and pluck
as he cleared the
speckled ground.

Now father told us daily
that
"Thanksgiving is quite near",
and
"Jehosaphat is looking good,
just fattening up the way he should."
Yes, our turkeys' fate
was clear....

We almost couldn't face him, or look him in the eye,
he seemed so extra friendly now,
we counted the days and wondered
how
we could ever say
"goodbye".

And mom, she planned the dinner
from the first bite to the
last
and she made a list of
guests to come,
(she'd add them up -
then 'add on' some)...
Thanksgiving was coming fast!

We were busy in the garden, picking corn and greens and herbs,
when the scrape of blade and 'sharpening stone'
came ringing 'round and made
us moan -
'Twas the time to kill our bird...

We tore past flapping linens, that
clung
to a mile of rope,
we trampled flowers, pushed a cow,
outran the dog, (though I don't know how),
as our feet flew high
on hope...

"Jehosaphat...we're coming....!
Jehosaphat's our friend.....!"

And father stood with blade in hand,
the turkey
blinked -
(did he understand),
'twas the moment of his
end?

Now that day is long behind us,
and we've realized every wish...
as Jehosaphat still runs about,
though mother's crabby
and
tends to shout -
'Cause she served
Thanksgiving
fish.

The Last Chance Dance

The night had arrived, and
dead
or alive,
NO QUESTION - I'd just have
to go...
T'was the year end dance - and
my very last chance,
(only men - only mice, could
know!)

Now mom was invited, (she sure was
excited,
she'd worked hard and long all
the day).
While we walked there together,
I wondered at whether
the OTHER GUYS'
MOTHERS
would stay...

Now we stood in the gym
and the lights, they were dim,
and the girls, all the girls,
they
did smile.

Then mom found a chair, and
I left her right there,
and she said,
"I'll just watch for
a while..."

The music was blaring, we stood
around staring,
'THE APPROACH', we all knew, was the key.
And there before others, and everyone's
mother,
a girl
yes
A GIRL,
she asked
ME!

I gulped and said "NO" - she said "CHICKEN, let's
go..."
I was cornered, now what
could I do?
But it wasn't as bad, as the nightmares
I'd had,
though my mom was still watching -
it's true...

'Round the floor I did groove
and I tried my best moves,
feeling confidence rush to my head.
Then the D.J. announced,
and quite clearly pronounced,
"UP NEXT is a SLOW DANCE,
INSTEAD..."
Now brave men have fainted, their courage though tainted,
at the prospect of similar tasks.
But this was the dance, and my
very last chance -
and before me - the girl who had
asked.

'Round her waist went my arms, and
I watched, though alarmed,
as her hands, on my shoulders, did
go,
and I stepped and I stepped
(on her feet I suspect)
Then the D.J. yelled
"SNOWBALL...",
(Oh, NO...!)

The world, it meant trading, no questions, debating,
all partners, they switched with another.
And my very last chance, at the
very last dance,
was a dance, with my very
own
MOTHER...

My Best Castle

(The sandbox is our favorite place
we play the morning long,
my brothers castles are the
best,
but
mine just turn out wrong.

The towers and the bridge
collapse -
I end up with a square,
the sand just slips and
slides
away
'till almost nothing's
         there.)

Now in the neighbour's yard next door,
some men were working 'round.
They left some powdered white
cement
in bags upon the ground.

The answer to my problems - clear -
I'd mix the powder in...
but when my brother sat
too
close,
I poured it over him.

He smiled and blinked his eyes of
blue,
his body covered white.
I gave a yell for mom to
help -
he looked an awful sight!

Now mom she thought it
terrible...
"what ever shall we do?
This stuff is even up his
nose,
all through his clothing
too..."
She lifted him
quite carefully,
and to the bathroom ran,
she poured a bubbly, steamy
bath,
"lets wash off...what we can!"

But somehow mom, she did
forget;
cement and water mix,
they harden right before your
eyes
into a solid fix.

My brothers hair stood tall
and spiked,
his eyebrows lumpy balls,
the muscles on his arms were LARGE -

(they use to be quite small).

We giggled as we chipped away,
(at last I'd had success!)

'Cause now of all my castles
built,
HE
had to be my BEST!

Static Cling

I didn't have socks, a top or some
pants,
not underthings, over things too,
'cause mom had washed
all
of my clothes...
now WHAT
could I possibly do?

My dresser was empty, my closet was
bare,
I only had P.J.'s and shoes.
The school bus was coming,
just
minutes away,
"Hey mom...I've a
QUESTION
for you...

Where's all my
stuff?
I've NOTHING TO WEAR,
I can't go to school, I'm undressed!"

"It's all in the hamper", she called back to me,
"all folded and sorted and
pressed!"

So down to the laundry room, quickly
I ran,
and I grabbed up a handful, or more.
I jumped into this
and I buttoned up
that,
and dashed
with my books, out the door.
Now mom had forgotten (in all of the rush),
and I had forgotten it too -
that staticy cling was a problem with
us
and clothes stuck together like
glue.

So off to the bus and to school
I did go...
with some underpants
stuck
to my back,
and my 'friends', they all questioned,

"Lost something today?"

But I wouldn't admit -
not to
THAT!

Teddy and Perks

Young Teddy and Perks were brothers,
and they lived in Ludlow Town.
They'd venture 'bout most summer days,
walk the old road down a ways
explore the farmland 'round.

Far over the grassy hilltops
and 'cross the fields they ran,
pulling arms of yellow wheat
and falling down in breathless
heaps
playing Catch Me, If You
Can...

Now, a brook they once
discovered,
flowing thick with speckled trout.
There 'pon the slippery rocks
they'd stand, and reach with
twigs and gentle hand,
to tickle the fish
about.

And a farmer's wife, she saw
them
as they passed her cottage gate,
"come Master Teddy and Master Perks,
drink of cider to quench your thirst and
try my butter milk cakes".

There, they sat 'neath oak and blossom,
while the farmer's wife did sing.
Her eyes ashine with wink and grin,
she spun her tales and drew them in -
to the lives of neighbours and kings.

Then off -
to Park Hall Manor; abandoned, ancient
grounds,
where ivy stems grew
thick as trees, the walls of stone
were cloaked in leaves,
and cattle
milled around.

The perfect secret club house,
the perfect spies retreat.
They'd climb and slide the mossy
bricks,
and fashion swords and
brandish sticks
and challenge to Hide and
Seek.

Then a softness in the daylight -
the shadows angled
so,
would send the brothers fast abreast
with stories fair and filled
with
jest,
and off to home they'd
go.

Gizzard Skinning Time

I lay down, listened,
wiggled
scared.
My grandpa said,
"it's time...

I'm going to skin your
gizzard
now,
and possibly
I'll find
a rotten egg behind your
ear,
a candy by your chin...

It's quite an operation
this -
And now
we
will
begin..."

I giggled, but I shut my
eyes,
(I wasn't s'posed to see),

I heard some clangs, a slash of steel,
then
grandpa said to me,

"I have a touch that's delicate,
you've nothing
now
to fear -

That gizzard's clearly in my view,

...though

your
Funny Bone's
quite
 near..."

I almost let a laugh explode,
I almost rolled
about!

Then grandpa said, "your gizzard's
FINE,
no need to
take it
out!"

"But
look at this...

I've found a sweet -
it's
certainly not
mine!
Imagine that!
A lollipop!
It's
AMAZING
what you'll
find!"

My grandpa's gone now, 'cause
he died.
I miss his laugh
and grin.
I miss his pipe tobacco smell,
and the whiskers
on his chin.
I miss his stories by my bed,
and his naughty, silly rhymes,

but most of all,
I miss the fun
of
'Gizzard Skinning Time'.

Our Tea Party

Old carton among the lilies,
perfect table for our tea.
We covered it with lacey towels,
(if nanny finds them,
will she howl)
at Marjory and me!

Then blueberries we did gather
and rhubarb, sour and green.
We borrowed some cups of
porcelain fine,
we chose the best ones we could find,
(so 'good' they're NEVER SEEN).

Then I mixed some raspberry tea
leaves
and water from the well.
We set the table for our guests,
they wore their bonnets and Sunday
Best,
and I rang the 'tea time' bell.

"Oh isn't it quite lovely - such a
perfect time of year!"

and we raised our pinky fingers,
spoke of how the summer lingers,
and "how nice you look, my dear..."

We ate the tiny berries 'till our
teeth and lips turned blue,
and Marjory sucked a rhubarb stalk
until she nearly couldn't talk -
('course, she'd say, "it isn't true!")

Then we made some chocolate mud pies,
and we baked them in the sun.
We watched a thousand ants go
by,
they danced a line across
our pies,
and we couldn't eat but
one.

Then Marjory's doll got hiccups
and she fell upon the ground.
We washed her with a bit of tea -
she looked alright, (it seemed to
me),
but, Marjory only
frowned.

Now we've tucked away the carton
just behind our favorite tree,
and we've had a spoon of medicine -
'cause nanny said "you'd better, when
you've had a fill of rhubarb
with your blueberries and tea."

When Ooffie Met Lion

Ooffie was so very small
a little ball
of long haired fur, that
dragged upon the ground
and flipped up, tipped up
with a straight centre part, and two
pink bows -
like a lady's coif,
(very soft, you know).
And she would race around
on tiny legs
you couldn't see.
Floating, hovering,
(like a water bug
discovering
a brand new pond...)

And could she jump!
Like an athlete - FLY!
She'd spring as high
as five foot four,
or even more!
She was Maltese by style and
type -
a snippet of a dog;
mouse-like.

And was Ooffie BRAVE!
Not a single fear displayed -
she'd growl and race,
give chase to a four ton
truck,
a train, or
(as you'll see) even
LION,
A great Dane.

Now to understand THIS
dog,
(the Dane, who's name
was
Lion),
you have to think BIG
like a horse, or cow,
(just picture somehow
a dog that you can ride upon
like at the fair
or circus ground - around and around.
I mean, not only YOU,
but then as well,
a friend or two!)

He had warm and droopy
gentle eyes, and
he wore no fanciful
disguise
to a dear and timid nature.
And Oh boy, was
he
a COWARD!
Frightened through and through
of a clapping hand, a cough, the
dropping of a
shoe.
He'd just disappear,
clear out -
underneath a table, behind a chair
or door.
And poor Lion, had no roar -
He'd whimper
while he'd hide beneath his giant
paws,
head low and covered up
like a little pup.

Now Ooffie's human mom,
(her name was Mrs. Lyn)
was asked in quite a formal
way to
"come for tea" at the
residence

of Miss Marie.
"We shall attend",
proclaimed Mrs. Lyn, and
did begin
to reacily prepare
her precious one
for sandwiches and raspberry cream
and
fun.

But how
she did forget
one teensy, tiny thing -
that Miss Marie
did
happen just to be
the Mistress of "HIS HIGHNESS",
(LION),
I'll never know -
but it was so....

There was perhaps one
half moment
at the door,
when all was well -
But let me tell,
and picture if you can -

The awful stare,
the glare,
the flight of fluffy
fur,
as Ooffie chose her
target -
Lion's back -
and with a
SMACK
she landed.

Well,
T'was told the crashing trays of
sandwiches went on
for days and days,
and a hundred juicy raspberry
tarts
hung here and there like
Modern Art, upon
the walls at Miss Marie's.

(They were not asked
again
for tea...)

And
That's the story -
not easy to forget,
of
Ooffie and Lion,
and how and when
they
met.

Stitches

No one told me
no one said
they'd take a needle
and a long black
thread
and sew me up
like a button
or hem
when
brow and pavement met -
Yet
there stood
he,
with a pocket of pins, and
a measure of thread
and a wide toothed grin...

"It's not that bad..." I managed
to grunt -
"Just a tiny old cut - it's more
like a
bump..."
But a dribble of blood
betrayed my state,
and the man in white
said

"...WAIT...
I'm good at this - not a
slip or a miss,
just stitch and snip,
(won't hurt you a bit...)"

"Gee...I'm sorry..." I said,
(with tremendous regret),
"but...I've just got to
fly -
sure glad that we met -
but
GOODBYE!"

And that's when dad
he came to my aid,
and said
"Now son...we're BOTH going to stay -
And I'll tell you a story of a stitch or two
when I was a boy -
'bout the age of
you...

And a cow named
CARACAS
(she ran like a horse),
she raced me and chased me,
(didn't catch me of course...)
but I slid through a
fence hole
of wire (like thorns)
It pulled off my trousers and
my
'saddle'
got torn...

HEY...it wasn't THAT FUNNY!
well
maybe.....ok...
(though the worst was
'BEHIND ME'),
I
got stitches
that day!
...and a constant reminder,
from siblings and 'friends',
that a COW
named CARACUS
was the best
in the
end!"

"Thanks Dad..."
(I was grateful),
'cause the sewing was done,
...and we laughed our way homeward -
father,
stitches,
and
son.

The Contest

A cup sucking contest
was chosen,
'twas the test of the brave
and the strong,
and alongside my friends
in the bathroom
we took turns - until something
went wrong.

The idea
was to last 'for the longest' -
with a cup stuck to mouth and to chin,
and nothing could aid
the 'attachment'
but the action of
sucking
it
in.

Now the coolest of guys
were contenders
and they'd cheer and
they'd jostle and howl,
while each took a stab
at the 'title',
sucking hard - 'till they
'threw in the towel'...

When at last I was
ready to
try it -
I knew, yes
I knew
that I'd win -
and I sucked
on that cup with
a vengeance,
and
it wouldn't come off of my
chin......

Now my parents were having
a party,
there were relatives,
friends
'round the place.
And I stood in a panic
and wondered -
would they notice
a cup
on
my face?

Well I pulled and I pulled
and I popped it.
And I'll tell you
It felt pretty sore,
but the worst was the
'hickey' - like
marking
of a circular bruise
I now wore.

Would it pass as a
five o'clock shadow?
(Some whiskers could surely
be found?)
Or perhaps I'd pretend
some misfortune -
like falling...
flat out
on the ground.

But, alas,
I was destined for
laughter,
for flashbulbs and
photos and
jest.
And my chin will forever
be famous
as my cup sucking
proved to be
best.

Carolyn's Scary Story

**very scary - based on a fable

The midnight porch
was an island
adrift
in the nasty black,
as
Carolyn told us stories
that would curl our eyeballs back.

We'd ask her for fairies and fortunes,
for a bedtime fable or two...
And she'd smile with a smile
only sisters could smile,
and she'd say,
"I've a tale just
for you....

There was once an old woman,
Matilda,
who lived with her
husband,
a wretch -

And he'd loudly proclaim,
every night, 'twas the
same...
"I want liver... and onions...
NOW FETCH!"

And their fortune, it seems had long ended,
(their money jar, dusty, I fear...)
But the horrid old husband
demanded,
"Deliver my liver....
S' THAT CLEAR!"

Then he'd pound on the table so
fiercely, it would buckle
and bend, (now in two), and his wife in a
terrorized quandary,
couldn't think
of what EVER
she'd do...

T'was then
she remembered her cousin,
who had died (and was buried quite
near),
- would she miss just a piece of
her liver?
The answer seemed simple
and
clear...

With scarf wrapped around her;
concealing,
she took shovel and flashlight
and sack...
and she stole through the night to the graveyard.
And she DID IT,
and made her way back.

Now she fried up some spicy
old onions,
and she chopped all the liver quite
fine -
and she served up the steamy
hot dinner,
while her husband just bellowed -
"B'OUT TIME!"

Now pleased with her brilliance
and cunning,
the old woman did settle in bed,
but alas, in the night came the
noises,
A VOICE - whispered
softly and said......

"GIVE ME MY LIVER...I WANT IT...
GIVE ME MY LIVER...I SAY...
GIVE ME MY LIVER...YOU'VE GOT IT......
GIVE ME MY
LIVER..TODAY!"

Now, that's when our sister would leave us -
on the porch, in the dark of the night,
and she'd lock all the doors and the windows,
while we hollered with all of our might...

"Why, dear little brothers...."
she'd whisper, "Be quiet....now don't make a sound...
She's still searching, you know -
for her
LIVER -
she won't REST....NOT AT ALL....
'till it's FOUND..."

The Catch

To the middle of the bay
we rowed
one day,
with a pole, 6 worms and
a hook,
and we sat 'neath the sun,
while we watched
one by one
as the fish came to nibble
and look.

They were frisky and fine
and I wanted them
'mine'...
could a 'Fisherman'
I ever
be?
But they teased and they
danced,
tugged my line as they
pranced,
and they stole every worm
they could
see.

So we rowed back
distraught
o're the catch, never
caught,
and I crabbed about everything
near -
"That's a stupid old pole, and
they're
stupid old fish,
and I'll catch one
NOT EVER...
that's clear!"

With hook gleaming bare, I
dangled it there
just over the dock, in the lake,
and I sat in a pout, trying to figure things out,
"just where had I made my mistake?"

Then 'round swam a bass, and
he swallowed up
fast
every inch of the hook on my
line.
And there I stood proudly, proclaiming
quite loudly;

"I did it! I did it!...He's mine!"

When Gordie Went to Sea

He saw the raft -
a rubber raft, just sitting at the
shore.
He couldn't swim,
he needn't swim -
that's what the
raft
was for!
And that's how Gordie
went to sea,
one breezy afternoon,
and rode the swells on
high did he,
and lost the shoreline soon....

Now dad was strolling 'pon
the sands,
with Clooney bounding 'round.
He'd throw a stick into the waves
and SPLASH!...
the stick was found!
And mom was fixing sandwiches -
a picnic lunch
for all,
and we raced past
playing tag and
dash -
and "Can you catch the
ball?"

Now no one knew
'tis really true,
that Gordie'd gone to
sea.
We thought
he was just hiding
well -
(we'd find him soon, would we...)

Then in a crazed, determined gaze,
our Clooney gave a
HOWL -
she yelped and danced upon
the shore...
T'was surely something foul!

And twinkling 'pon horizons line,
just barely in his sight,
our father saw the rubber raft
and
hollered with his might,
"It's Gordie - son you're out too far...!"
and dived into the waves,
while straight behind him
Clooney pounced.....
T'was certain they were brave!

They cut the crest of giant surf
then
quickly disappeared -
and up,
then down,
then
up again,
t'was miles and miles they cleared!

Then Clooney faltered; tired, spent,
and clearly in distress -
swam straight towards our father's back,
(her only place to rest).
Now father was in trouble too...
how ever could he swim?
A heavy dog, a distant raft;
we'd have to rescue HIM!

'Twas father, son and dog
at sea,
on a summer afternoon.
We stood and wondered what to
do-
and best
to do it
soon!

Now, a neighbour, Mr. Weller,
he heard our desperate
pleas.
He flew, he splashed, he swam
on past,
and challenged the
rolling seas.

And we watched in hope
and horror,
and we held each breath (for days).
Could we see him -
NO!
Could we see him -
YES!
As he climbed each mountainous
wave.

And he reached the raft and
Gordie,
And he tugged with grit and
grin,
and he pulled and pulled, and
inch by inch,
he pulled that raft on in.

Then
father and Cloonie followed...
And all were safe ashore.
And we laughed and cried,
when Gordie sighed,
"Can I try that...
just once
more...?"

Down Yi

* (Yi is pronounced like "Hi")

"Ten big
very good potatoes,"
Dad asked me to
fetch,
"do you mind...?"
And he pointed to the
door
of the cellar,
"Down Yi...
'tis the best you will
find..."

And I gulped
in thinking of
the cellar,
where the walls
held spiders
and
more.
And I wanted
quite truly
to go down
there,
(but
I'd trouble,
yes, trouble
with the door.)

"I think we've
potatoes
in the pantry..
and we should, (mother says),
use them first..."

"But the stew needs
THE BEST
for its flavor,
and I fear..."
said my dad,
"they're the worst!"

So I managed,
(though in
truth, 't wasn't easy.)
And I opened up
the door
leading down.
And I switched on
the dim light
to guide me
and
I stepped
to the cellar, 'neath
the ground.

There was wet
in the cold air around
me,
and a smell
that was earthy
but clean.
And the shadows
of the bags and
the boxes,
were like
giants
just waiting
to be
seen.

"Are you coming now
Ut...?"
father called me...
"This pot is quite ready
for the spuds..."

And I ran to the
bag
in the corner,
and I grabbed
up the 'ten'
with a hug.

Now,
it took me less time
to go upstairs,
(I think it is shorter -
don't you?)
And I shut fast the
door to the cellar.
We had ten
good potatoes
for the
stew.

One More Time

Mom please tell me
one more time
before
I close my eyes,
the way you love me,
how you love me,
all the reasons
why.

I love to hear you
say the words, you
whisper softly so.
I love to listen when
you tell me
when you let me know -

I'm your darling

yes
your darling
even grown, and flown away -
like the sparrows in the
garden,
ever yours
in
every way.

Pogo

I begged
and I pleaded
I whined
that I needed
a puppy,
a puppy,
a pet of my own.

And yes, I would walk
him
in rain and
bad weather,
through storms and the
dark
of the park
near our home.

So Pogo, a Beagle
was purchased, made
legal,
with needles and name tags,
a collar and leash.
And dad bought him dog
food
in bags that were giant
and forty-five flavors
of biscuits
to eat.

The first day was frightful,
the night was a
night full
of mom in the yard with
umbrella and pup.
Then settled 'neath covers -
(my blankets discovered)
he snored
and he snored,
and he kept us
all up.

Now mom washed her stockings,
and hung them, (though blocking
the air vent, yes blowing
with heat all about.)
And Pogo,
(protecting)
our household from
wet things (?)
he HOWLED
and he HOLLERED
and chased them
right out!

He snitches the birdseed
from right
where the birds feed,
he finds my old bubblegum
stuck to the door.
He'll savor a shoe
lace,
regardless of true
taste
and won't eat his supper,
(he'll think it a bore).

And comedian ever,
our pup will
endeavour
to tackle the strangest, the
wildest
of tasks -
He'll chase his own
shadow, his tail
or reflection,
then cringe in detection
of
a bag floating past....

"I'll save you..!
I'll save you!"
(intentions
though true blue),
he'll challenge the lights
from
"the monster": our car,
(could it be his reaction
with
a burglar in action?)
...more likely a lick -
and
"you...like me...so far...?"

Or would he in boredom
just sigh
and ignore him,
"I'm sleepy...I'm resting...
please leave me alone!"
(I can picture it clearly,
he'd yawn,
most sincerely,
"come back a bit later...
when
someone's at
         home.........")

I thought I was happy
before this small puppy,
became a new member
yes, part of our home.
But now I know friendship -
that I can depend on,
and how I do love him -
this pup of my own.

The Mission

The great commando
gear in tow,
shoulders square,
not a hair
out of place,
was set to go.

His mission, tough;
a rescuing by plane,
then parachute
and swim (towards a raft with flashing light)
in ocean, grim and cold.
But, he was told
the plan was to unfold at midnight,
(could the time be
right?)

His muscles thick
and slick
with heavy sweat
he knew his job
and yet-
and yet-
he gulped quite
long and loud,
with great distress.....
was this a
TEST?

For all his missions
to this date
were in the daylight (though some
were
fairly late...)
But none,
(reviewed with careful
thought)
were
in the dark-
The time of monsters,
fearful things,
shadows, holes of black
to fall within,
and creatures slimy, dripping,
mucky, gross and
yucky, (and
after him!)

But this, his secret fear
was hidden well.
(And HE WOULD NEVER TELL!)

"Well Sir,...."
he said,
(the great commando to his boss,)
"I think this mission
is a loss -
It's far too risky...
not worth the awful chance
to life and limb...

And what a shame,
for
I
would love to rescue
the gentleman
in need."

"I knew
that you would understand the
risks at hand," said
he (the boss).
"I nearly
wrote this off -
But, yes I knew,
that only YOU
could follow through
with such a daring plan.

YES - YOU -
YOU are the man!"

"OH NO!", (a further gulp
went quickly down his gullet),
T'was surely stamped in
fate -
no chance to null it...
He would have to go,
to face the dark-
the black,
the deadly night.

...T'was destiny, all right!

He checked his watch
(computerized for seconds, minutes,
hours clear -
whether
on a distant, far off shore
or -
mearly
here, and
packed his flashlight
(with a longing look)
and
just in case -
a pack or two of "Forever Ready"
batteries
he took.

The plane was humming,
set for flight.
The great commando donned
his packaged chute
and sat within -
and
 so it did begin...
The Mission in
The Night.

Through clouded skies
without the moon to guide,
they flew a very bumpy ride,
and both the pilot
and commando (great)
felt gurgling aches
and
did agree
t'was yes, a (huge) mistake
to each partake of
triple burgers, fries and shake
before
the flight
but
hind sight was
too late - to see.

"NOW"
the bellowing voice proclaimed-
"JUMP!
the target's plain to me-
the ocean's down below,
NOW
GO! Upon the count of three!"

And out - out he dropped
DOWN
through the midnight air,
fast, then faster
did he go
towards the
wet below.
"Pull the cord..." he thought,
(as great commandos do),

UP,
the chute it shot -
to catch the wind
and slowly
drop him into the Giant Waves.

A mouth of salty water,
a nose full too,
the great commando knew
the job to do -

T'was SWIM!

Swim with all his might
towards...(what was it again?)
something -
something flashing in the night...

And there, submerged in blackness
all around,
the fear began to close about his throat
and he took note
of what did
seem to be
the
end.

T'was then, the great commando did
recall
the age old story
that said it all -
and in the ocean, dark and grave,
he did recite the lines,
with hope to save himself,
- so that he might complete
the rescuing -

(The Mission Thing)
and
face his boss.

He grit his teeth and with
defiance
he did toss the words
upon the fears that pressed around-
"I think I can, I think I can..."
and
bravely on
he
swam and swam.

There - there - he saw the light,
flashing, twinkling beacon in the night.
He powered on, (commandos have the might),
and there before him -
a tiny rubber boat
crashing about the waves
(but still afloat).

The great commando pulled
himself
aboard
and found a packet,
tucked and sealed against the floor.

Inside: a note in fancy script,
(plus chocolate bars, a can of juice,
an orange and soggy cracker bits.)

and 'pon the paper stated THUS:

> YOU WERE THE MISSION!
> AND THEREFORE
> HAVE SHOWN YOURSELF (AND US) THAT
> YOU HAVE FACED YOUR FEARS,
> (WE KNEW THEM ALL ALONG!)
> AND ONLY WHEN YOU FACED THE
> DARK -
> COULD YOU BE TRULY STRONG!
> AND NOW YOU CAN DO ANYTHING -
> ANYTHING AT ALL!
> NO TASK TOO LARGE (OR SMALL) -
> CONGRATULATIONS! WELL DONE, I SAY...!
> (and now,
> t's clear that you should
> make your way
> HOME-
> GOOD LUCK...!)

"OH!"
thought the great (and brave) commando -,
as he paddled with his muscled arms -
He ate a chocolate bar,
and looked upon the waters far....
the journey would be very long -

"I think I can....
I think I can...

he whispered softly, paddling on
into
the night.

PRINTED BY
IMPRIMERIE D'ÉDITION MARQUIS
IN DECEMBER 1995
MONTMAGNY (QUÉBEC)